I Can Be Anything!

I CAN BE A LIBRARIAN

By Anthony Ardely

Please visit our website, www.garethstevens.com. For a free color catalog of all our high-quality books, call toll free 1-800-542-2595 or fax 1-877-542-2596.

Cataloging-in-Publication Data

Names: Ardely, Anthony.
Title: I can be a librarian / Anthony Ardely.
Description: New York : Gareth Stevens Publishing, 2019. | Series: I can be anything! | Includes index.
Identifiers: LCCN ISBN 9781538217627 (pbk.) | ISBN 9781538217603 (library bound) | ISBN 9781538217634 (6 pack)
Subjects: LCSH: Librarians–Juvenile literature. | Libraries–Juvenile literature.
Classification: LCC Z682.A73 2019 | DDC 020.92–dc23

First Edition

Published in 2019 by
Gareth Stevens Publishing
111 East 14th Street, Suite 349
New York, NY 10003

Editor: Kate Mikoley
Designer: Laura Bowen

Photo credits: Cover, p. 1 (kid) nataliya/Shutterstock.com; cover, p.1 (background) Andersen Ross/Blend Images/Getty Images; pp. 5, 13, 23, 24 wavebreakmedia/Shutterstock.com; pp. 7, 17 Tyler Olson/Shutterstock.com; pp. 9, 11 asiseeit/E+/Getty Images; pp. 15, 24 hxdbzxy/Shutterstock.com; p. 19 Education Images/Universal Images Group/Getty Images; p. 21 IMAGEMORE Co, Ltd./Getty Images.

Printed in the United States of America

CPSIA compliance information: Batch #CS18GS: For further information contact Gareth Stevens, New York, New York at 1-800-542-2595.

Contents

Librarians love to read!
I do, too!

They work with books.

Ms. Poe is a librarian.
She helps my class.

Welcome!
My name is
Susan

She helps us find books we like.

Welcome!

We find them
on the shelf.

We find them on
the computer.

You can take books home. Librarians check them out.

You need to
bring them back.
This is called borrowing.

NEW YORK PUBLIC LIBRARY
Book Drop
New York
Public
Library
New York
Public
Library

I borrow this one.
It's about spiders!

J1
SPIDERS: EIGHT-LEGGED TERRORS

I can be a librarian.
So can you!

Words to Know

computer

shelf

Index